THE CONJUROR'S COOKBOOK
GHOSTLY GOULASH

JONATHAN EMMETT

ILLUSTRATED BY
COLIN PAINE

BLOOMSBURY
CHILDREN'S
BOOKS

For Caitlin – J.E.
For Celia and John – C.P.

First published in Great Britain in 2000
Bloomsbury Publishing Plc, 38 Soho Square, London, W1V 5DF

Copyright © Text Jonathan Emmett 2000
Copyright © Illustrations Colin Paine 2000

The moral right of the author has been asserted
A CIP catalogue record of this book is available from the
British Library

ISBN 0 7475 4413 1

Printed in England by Clays Ltd, St Ives plc

10 9 8 7 6 5 4 3 2 1

Jake's granny was the most extraordinary cook. She could cook anything and everything. So, when Great Aunt Elinor sent her a strange book full of magical recipes, she didn't think twice about trying them out.

It was just as well that Jake was there to help out – you never know what might happen when you open The Conjuror's Cookbook.

Clobber and Snatchett

Jake was very excited. He was going to spend another weekend cooking at Granny's cottage – not just ordinary cooking. They were going to make something special – a magic recipe from The Conjuror's Cookbook!

Jake and Granny had used the cookbook twice before and they knew that it could get them into all sorts of trouble. But the recipes were so exciting that they couldn't wait to try another one.

So Jake was surprised to find Granny looking pale and unhappy. She'd forgotten all about cooking. She'd even forgotten that she'd invited him to stay.

'What's the matter?' he asked.

'They're going to throw me out of my cottage,' said Granny, bursting into tears, 'and bring a bulldozer to knock it down.'

'Who are?'

'Clobber and Snatchett,' sobbed Granny, pulling a crumpled letter out of her apron. 'They're businessmen. They want to build a new shopping centre here.'

Jake read the letter slowly. It was very complicated and he didn't understand all of it, but it seemed that Granny was right. It said that the cottage had to be knocked down to make room for a drive-through take-away.

'But they can't just throw you out. Not if you don't want to go.'

'Well, that's what I've been telling them,' sniffed Granny, 'but they're coming round this evening and they say that they've found a way to get rid of me.'

'When are they coming?'

'Six o'clock.'

'But that's now,' said Jake. And someone began hammering on the front door.

Granny opened the door and gasped as a huge man barged past her into the cottage. She was so taken aback by the intruder, she didn't notice a second man, small and pinch-faced, scuttle in after him.

'Ahem,' coughed the little man, trying to

attract Granny's attention. 'Mrs Baker, I presume.'

Granny was still gaping up at the huge man who was looming menacingly above her. She couldn't believe that he'd fitted through the doorway.

Jake decided to answer on her behalf.

'You seem to "presume" rather a lot,' he said. 'No one said you could come in.'

'Oh, I beg your pardon,' sneered the little

man, 'but time is money and we can't afford to waste it. I'm Mr Snatchett and this is my partner, Mr Clobber. We're here to –'

'I know why you're here,' interrupted Jake. 'Granny's told me all about you. And she's not leaving this cottage, no matter what you say.'

'She doesn't have any choice,' snapped Mr Snatchett. 'You see, we've been keeping an eye on this cottage and we know a thing or two about it.'

'Like what?' asked Granny, coming to her senses.

'Like that it's a danger to the en-vir-on-ment,' grunted Clobber, stumbling over the word.

'It's a *what*?' asked Jake.

'It's all been properly documented,' said Snatchett, handing them another letter.

Granny took the letter and they read through it slowly.

It claimed that Granny was carrying out

dangerous and illegal experiments that were threatening the countryside. There were accounts of a strange soup flood, a huge earth-shaking explosion, a low-flying jet-propelled saucepan and a startling smell that had caused dozens of accidents in a nearby town. The letter finished by saying that unless Granny moved out of the cottage, they would report her to the police and she would be thrown into prison.

It was true, of course. All these things had happened when Jake and Granny had tried out recipes from The Conjuror's Cookbook. No real harm had come of them, but the police wouldn't see it that way.

It looked as if Granny would be forced to move out after all!

A Box Full of Magic

'That's blackmail!' said Granny.

'That's ridiculous!' said Jake, giving her a sharp nudge. 'I mean, *soup floods*, *jet-propelled saucepans*! Do you think anyone will take that nonsense seriously?'

Granny gaped at Jake for a moment and then she caught on.

'Quite right!' she said. 'And as for strange smells and explosions, well, any fool can see that this is just a cottage, not a chemical factory. You've just made all this up.'

'Have we?' grunted Clobber, scratching his head.

'Of course not, you idiot,' hissed Snatchett. 'You saw it with your own eyes.'

'Can you prove that?' said Jake defiantly.
The two men frowned at each other.

'No,' blurted Clobber, 'but –'

'Shut up and get back in the van,' barked
Snatchett, herding his partner out of the
door.

'OK, so you can stay a little longer,' he
said, turning back, 'but we'll get rid of
you, one way or another.'

'We'll see about that,' said Granny and
she slammed the door in his face.

'That showed them!' said Jake, when the
two men had driven off.

'For now,' said Granny, shaking her
head, 'but they'll be back.'

'Well it's still worth celebrating. And I
know just the way to do it.'

'How?'

'By cooking something *special*!' said Jake,
pulling the The Conjuror's Cookbook
down from the shelf. 'Isn't that why I'm
here?'

'I'd forgotten all about that,' admitted Granny.

'Well I haven't!' said Jake enthusiastically. 'So have you got some more *magic* ingredients?'

'I've got dozens,' said Granny, fetching a battered package from the larder. 'Your Great Aunt Elinor sent me a whole box full, just before this trouble started.'

Great Aunt Elinor was Granny's elder sister. She was an explorer and spent all

her time travelling around the far-flung corners of the world. She had come across the cookbook on her travels and had promised to keep an eye out for the magic ingredients needed for its recipes.

'So what have we got?' asked Jake excitedly.

'I don't know. I've been too busy worrying about the cottage to take a proper look.'

They opened the box and found that it was stuffed full of tiny packets and bottles.

'Witchroot, fairy flour, spookweed, trollberries,' said Granny, reading the labels.

'There's even some more bogey beans,' said Jake, holding up a packet.

'I don't think we'll be needing those,' said Granny. 'Not after the mess the Goblins made last time.'

'I bet we could cook dozens of recipes with these,' said Jake, picking up the cookbook.

Even the book seemed to be excited. Jake

could feel the cover pulsing beneath his fingers. It fluttered its pages, one way and then the other, showing off all the wonderful recipes that it had to offer.

'Now hold on a minute,' said Granny. 'Don't get too carried away. There's still a bit of a problem.'

'What?'

'Well, we've got plenty of magic ingredients, but we've hardly got any ordinary ones. I haven't been shopping for ages. I was terrified that I'd come back and find that the cottage had been knocked down.'

'So what have you got?'

'Well, nothing really,' said Granny, 'just a bit of flour, an ancient turnip and an old jar of paprika. I've been getting really hungry.'

'Just our luck,' groaned Jake.

It was nearly seven o'clock. By the time they got to the supermarket, it would be closed. He'd got all excited about using the

cookbook, but now he'd have to wait until morning.

'Hang on a minute,' said Granny. 'I think the book's trying to show us something.'

The book was flapping its pages, trying to attract their attention.

'You don't suppose it's got a recipe for us?' said Jake. 'One we can do, without having to go shopping.'

'I shouldn't be surprised,' admitted Granny.

They picked up the book and this is what they read.

Ghostly Goulash

Ivan Unger, Transylvania's great Tomato Sorcerer, invented this recipe. It's surprisingly filling and guaranteed to raise the spirits.

INGREDIENTS
A bit of flour
An ancient turnip
An old jar of paprika
A handful of powdered spookweed
A large dollop of tomato sorcery

Put the tomato sorcery into a pan and stir awake. Once woken, leave for as long as you dare and then add flour until settled. Bring the pan to the boil and simmer while you prepare the rest of the ingredients.

The turnip should be really ancient and wrinkly. The best ones are almost fossilised with a few dinosaur teeth-marks here and there. If your turnip is less than twenty years old, you might as well not bother.

Cut the turnip into thin slices. Lick each slice on both sides and then turn it over in the spookweed until it has an even coating.

Toss the coated slices into the pan, remembering to stand well back and wear sunglasses.

Stir in the paprika and bring the pan back to the boil. Then cover and simmer for thirty minutes before serving.

'Well,' said Jake, 'shall we give it a try?'

Granny wasn't too sure. She had nearly lost the cottage as a result of following the cookbook's other recipes.

'Come on,' urged Jake. 'It says it's "guaranteed to raise the spirits", and you need cheering up.'

'Oh, all right,' said Granny, smiling at last. 'I am starving. Let's give it a go!'

Jake searched through the magic ingredients until he found a packet of spookweed and a bottle of tomato sorcery. The bottle was pointed and covered in silver stars like a wizard's hat.

'Here we are,' said Granny, fetching the

other ingredients. The turnip certainly looked ancient. It was as wrinkled as a walnut.

'Do you think it's more than twenty years old?' asked Jake.

'I should imagine so,' said Granny. 'I found it down the back of one of the cupboards. I think it's been here longer than I have.'

'Let's go then!'

Jake opened the bottle and let a large

dollop of red sauce roll sluggishly into a
pan.

Granny took a wooden spoon and gave
it a little stir.

'Did you hear that?' Jake asked.

'Hear what?'

'The sauce! I think it's making a noise.'

They put their ears next to the saucepan
and heard a faint murmuring sound.

Granny stirred a little more and the
sauce let out a long yawn and stretched
across the bottom of the pan.

'Well I never!' said Granny, dropping the
spoon.

'It must be awake,' said Jake.

The sauce grunted a bit and began
rolling around the bottom of the pan,
sloshing against the sides as it built up
speed. After a minute or so, it began
whooping and splashing up above the rim.
Jake gasped as dollops of sauce shot into
the air, exploded like fireworks and fell,
shrieking, back into the pan.

'I think we'd better add the flour now,' said Granny. 'Before any sauce escapes.'

Jake sprinkled on some flour and the sauce quietened down a bit. He added a bit more and the sauce let out a sigh and settled down in the bottom of the pan.

'That's it,' said Jake. And he set the pan to simmer.

Next, Granny took a sharp knife and cut up the turnip, passing the slices to Jake who licked each one before coating it in spookweed.

When all the slices were done, Granny fetched some sun-glasses.

'They're not very trendy,' she admitted, handing Jake a pair with pink flowery frames. 'But they're all I've got.'

'Here goes then,' said Jake, and he tossed the first slice into the pan.

Flash-Bang-Dollop!

The slice flew through the air and there
was a blinding flash and a deafening bang
as it landed in the saucepan.

'Blimey!' gasped Jake. It was as if a bolt
of lightning had struck inside the kitchen.

'Never mind sun-glasses,' said Granny.
'What about ear-plugs?'

Jake tossed the rest of the slices into the
pan. Each had the same effect. It was like
standing at the centre of a thunderstorm,
only it wasn't raining.

'Wow!' said Jake, when he had finished.
'That was better than fireworks.'

'Pardon?' said Granny, who was still
getting her hearing back.

They stirred in the paprika, set the pan to

simmer and then tidied up while they
were waiting.

'Time's up!' said Granny at last.
  She fetched two bowls, intending to pour
a helping into each. But the goulash was
incredibly thick. It rolled into the first bowl
in one big dollop. She tried to spoon some
of it into the other bowl, but she couldn't.
It flowed off the spoon as soon as she lifted

'It looks like we'll have to share,' said Granny.

'I'm not sure that we should eat it,' said Jake. 'It looks a bit odd.'

'Please yourself,' said Granny, 'I'm starving.'

She lifted the bowl and sniffed it.

'Interesting,' she said and took a sip from the edge. But then her eyes nearly popped out of her head as the goulash squirmed out of the bowl and into her mouth in one great gooey glob.

Granny made a long gulping noise as the goulash slipped straight down into her stomach.

'Goodness!' she said, catching her breath. 'I wasn't expecting that. Now I know what the book means by "surprisingly filling". It feels like I just swallowed an elephant.'

'What did it taste like?' asked Jake.

'A bit peculiar, but nothing special. I don't know why the recipe said that it would "raise the spirits". I feel a little gassy, if anything.'

Granny sat back in her chair and rubbed her tummy, frowning.

'Oh dear,' she groaned. 'It's getting worse. Excuse me, but I'm going to have to –'

Granny let out a long wet burp. And as she did so, the most extraordinary thing happened.

A ghost swam out of her mouth!

The ghost wore nothing but a pair of sandals and a long white sheet, draped loosely over one shoulder.

He hung motionless above the kitchen table, his head tilted back and his arms spread at his sides.

Jake and Granny gaped at him for some time before he muttered out the corner of his mouth, 'Go on, clap.'

'Clap?' repeated Jake hesitantly.

'Applaud my entrance!' said the ghost,

throwing his head back further. 'I'm giving you my Julius Caesar.'

'Oh, thank you very much,' said Jake. He and Granny clapped uncertainly and the ghost dropped his pose and floated down beside them.

'That's more like it,' he said. 'For one ghastly moment, I thought you didn't recognise me.'

'Err, should we?' asked Granny.

'You mean you don't?' said the ghost in a hurt tone. 'I'm Samuel Poopshank, the

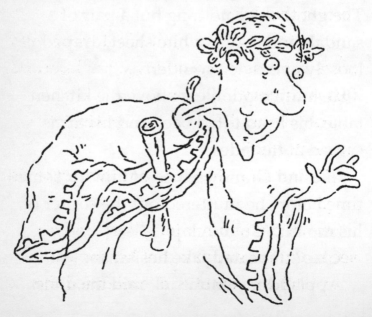

famous actor. I've trod the boards of Europe's finest theatres. I've worked with Shakespeare.'

'*With* Shakespeare?' repeated Jake.

'Yes,' said Samuel grandly, 'you must have heard of him.'

'I think so,' admitted Jake. 'He's dead, isn't he?'

'For about the last four hundred years,' agreed Granny.

'Really?' said Samuel looking downcast. 'What a tragedy. I hadn't realised I'd been resting that long.'

'I'm afraid so,' said Jake, 'but we're very pleased to meet you anyway. I'm Jake and this is Granny.'

Granny nodded, but was looking uncomfortable.

'Pardon me,' she said, 'but I've got to do it again.'

She let out another long burp and a second ghost swam out of her mouth.

'A kitchen – excellent!' exclaimed the

new ghost, looking around him. He was dressed as a chef and holding a large meat cleaver.

'Is this where you keep all the food,' he asked, floating straight into the larder.

'Err, usually,' said Granny, running after him, 'but –'

'Empty!' wailed the chef, floating back out.

Granny would have said something about not poking your nose into other people's larders, but all she could manage was another burp.

This time, a huge woman swam out. She was dressed as a ballet-dancer, but was so fat, it would be a wonder if she could run, let alone dance.

'Hello,' she said, straining into a curtsey, 'I'm Trixibelle. You couldn't whip up a sandwich for me, could you? I'm absolutely famished.'

'Me too!' chorused the other ghosts.

Ghostly Guests

It seemed that all the ghosts had met their deaths while ravenously hungry.

Samuel, the actor, hadn't eaten because he was nervous about his first night playing Julius Caesar. Unfortunately, there had been a mix-up with the props and he'd ended up being stabbed with real daggers instead of pretend ones.

The chef, whose name was Alexis, was allergic to garlic, but had found himself working around the clock in a posh French restaurant where they put garlic in everything. He'd gone without eating anything for two days before being killed by a gas explosion.

And Trixibelle, the enormous ballet-dancer, was on the second day of a strict diet when she took a big jump and crashed to her death through an old stage floor.

But it didn't stop there. Granny kept burping up more and more hungry ghosts.

There was an explorer who'd been buried in an avalanche after setting off into the mountains without enough provisions; a pirate whose shipmates had forced him to walk the plank after he'd fed the last ship's biscuit to the cat; and an African cannibal who'd decided to become a vegetarian and ended up being eaten himself.

And they were just the first few. The kitchen was soon thronging with ghosts, all clamouring for food.

'They can't stay here,' said Granny, fighting back another burp. 'They're bound to cause trouble. We have to get rid of them.'

'Don't you have to put their souls to rest?' said Jake, remembering a television

programme he'd seen about ghosts.

'You should feed us!' explained Alexis the chef. 'We were all too hungry to die properly. We'll be stuck here haunting this cottage until we get a decent meal.'

'Yes, give us some food!' shouted the others.

'But I don't have any,' pleaded Granny.

'I've got an idea,' said Jake, fetching Granny's telephone directory. 'Here we are, "Donald's Dial-A-Pizza"! We'll get some food delivered!'

It was more than an hour before the doorbell rang, by which time Granny was weak with burping and the downstairs rooms were teaming with spooks of every description.

Jake shooed the ghosts into the kitchen and opened the front door.

A tiny deliveryman was struggling beneath a teetering tower of pizza boxes.

'Pizzas for Mrs Baker,' whined a voice from behind the dark visor of the man's motorcycle helmet. He looked very

peculiar. His uniform was far too big for him and was bunched up around his wrists and ankles.

There was a lot of noise coming from the kitchen, where Granny was having a hard time keeping the ghosts in.

'Who've you got back there, then?' asked the man, trying to peek over Jake's shoulder.

Jake took the pizzas and stuffed some money into the man's hand.

'Just my Granny,' he said, trying to shut the door. 'You can keep the change.'

'Oh no, I won't hear of it,' said the man, jamming his foot in the door. 'Here you go.'

The man slowly counted out the change while bobbing up and down, trying to get another glance over Jake's shoulder.

'I think that's the right money now, thank you,' said Jake impatiently. He shoved the man's boot out of the door and managed to close it, just before a line of ghosts plopped straight through the wall behind him.

'Food! Food!' cried the ghosts, grabbing the pizza boxes.

'I'm sorry,' said Granny, coming through the doorway. 'I couldn't hold them any longer. Do you think he saw them?'

'I don't think so,' said Jake, 'but he was acting a bit odd.'

The ghosts tore open the boxes and stuffed the pizza into their mouths. But instead of disappearing, the slices just fell through their bodies and onto the floor. The ghosts picked up the pizza and tried to eat it again, but the same thing happened. This made the ghosts even hungrier.

'Oh dear,' said Jake disappointedly. 'I should have guessed it wouldn't be that simple.'

Granny didn't say anything. She just slumped onto the stairs and belched out a zookeeper.

An Unwelcome Visitor

The deliveryman walked up the lane and climbed into a black van that was parked in the shadows.

'See anything?' grunted a voice.

'Not a sausage,' snarled Snatchett, taking off the helmet.

The sneaky businessmen had waylaid the real deliveryman and paid him off, taking his uniform and helmet before sending him home.

'But they're up to something. That's for sure.'

'What now then?' grunted Clobber.

'Wait until dark,' said

Snatchett, 'then take a closer look.'

It wasn't until the hall clock had struck midnight that Granny was able to stop burping. By which time the cottage was overrun with ghosts.

Most had fallen asleep, but many of them still hung around the kitchen moaning about how hungry they were. There were now so many ghosts that some of them had to share the same space. Trixibelle, the fat ballet-dancer, had a

highwayman *and* a tiny headmistress sitting inside her, like a set of Russian dolls. And all three of them were groaning about their empty stomachs.

Granny sat at the kitchen table, clutching her head.

'I don't know how much longer I can stand this,' she said. 'I might have to move out after all.'

'Don't be silly,' said Jake. 'We'll think of something.'

The moon was very bright that night and, had the curtains not been drawn, Jake and Granny might have spotted someone sneaking around outside. A ladder was resting against the wall of the cottage and someone was climbing through Granny's bedroom window.

The intruder had just lowered himself to the floor when there was a terrific screech. He had trodden on Delia, Granny's cat, who had been sleeping on the floor.

The intruder leapt sideways and moonlight poured into the dark room, revealing a sea of sleeping ghosts stretching all around him. Or at least they *had* been sleeping. Delia's screech had woken them all up.

'Food! Food!' moaned the ghosts, as they stirred awake.

The intruder was terrified. Being surrounded by a roomful of ghosts was bad enough. But when he saw Alexis staring up at him, holding a meat cleaver, he had the horrible feeling that he was going to be the first course in some ghoulish midnight feast.

He scrambled towards the door, but skidded to a halt as the cannibal reared up in front of it.

'Mummy! Help!' he squealed, as he fled back across the room and leapt, recklessly, out of the window.

'What on earth is going on?' said Granny, as she rushed in with Jake.

'Beats me,' said Alexis. 'I woke up and found someone standing in my stomach. The next thing I know he's throwing himself out the window.'

'Speaking of stomachs,' said Samuel, 'have you found anything to put in ours yet?'

'Look at this!' said Jake, picking up a camera which the intruder had abandoned.

'And these!' said Granny, pointing to the huge muddy footprints that ran across the carpet. They could only think of one

person who wore boots that big.

'Clobber!' said Jake. 'But what was he doing here?'

'I don't know, but I'm sure that he was up to no good.'

They looked out of the window into the garden, but the intruder was long gone.

Snatchett Sneaks
a Peek

Jake went to bed, but Granny stayed up to keep an eye on the ghosts. She didn't want them wandering outside where Clobber or Snatchett might photograph them.

So she was only half-awake when she pulled open the kitchen curtains the next morning. She didn't think to check if anyone was outside.

'Aha!' exclaimed Snatchett. The little man was standing on a box, looking straight into the kitchen.

'Gadzooks!' gasped Samuel, who was sitting beside the window.

'A ghost!' said Snatchett triumphantly. 'So Clobber *was* right. Well you might have scared him off but you won't get rid of me!'

'Get out of my garden!' shouted Granny angrily. 'Or I'll call the police.'

'Don't bother,' sneered Snatchett, 'I'll fetch them myself. There's an ancient by-law against *raising the dead* and the punishment is death!'

'What's he doing here?' asked Jake, running into the kitchen. 'And where's Clobber?' he added suspiciously.

'He's taking an early retirement,' said Snatchett, 'in Australia. He wanted to get as far away from this cottage as possible.'

'Good,' said Jake. 'Why don't you go with him.'

'What,' taunted Snatchett, 'and miss all the fun? I'm going now, but I'll be back later, with the police!'

He jumped off the box and scuttled out of the garden.

'Well, that's it then,' sighed Granny. 'I'm

done for. The police will find the cottage crawling with ghosts and I'll probably be burnt at the stake.'

'No you won't,' said Jake, trying to sound reassuring. 'They don't do that any more. Do they?'

Granny sank into a chair and looked miserable.

Even the ghosts forgot about their empty stomachs and fell silent.

But Jake wasn't ready to give up yet. He paced around the kitchen trying to think of a way out.

'Of course,' he exclaimed at last. 'I can't believe we didn't think of it before!'

'What?' asked Granny.

'The Conjuror's Cookbook!' said Jake. 'It's bound to have a recipe that will help us!'

Jake pulled the book down from the shelf and it snapped open immediately. He felt like kicking himself. If they hadn't tidied the book away, it could have helped them earlier.

'Here we are,' he said, reading out loud.

'Golem Bread

This bread has a character of its own and, although too insubstantial for the human stomach, will more than satisfy those of a fainter constitution.'

'Brilliant,' said Granny. 'What do we need to cook it?'

'Just flour and water,' said Jake. 'And something called yiddle yeast. That must be the magic ingredient.'

'Here it is,' said Granny, producing a small purple packet from Great Aunt Elinor's box. 'And we've got some flour left over from the goulash.'

'Brilliant,' said Jake, 'we can bake it right now.'

The recipe was like that for ordinary bread, except for the special yiddle yeast, which

was so soft and weightless, it was almost
as if it wasn't there.

Granny whistled cheerfully as she
prepared the dough. She was still worried
about Snatchett, but she was never happier
than when she was cooking, and right
now, that was the best thing for her to do.

As soon as the ghosts realised that
Granny was making something that they
could actually eat, they all crowded into
the kitchen, filling the room like a fog.
Granny felt uncomfortable walking

through their bodies, but she couldn't avoid it.

'Excuse me,' she said, as she slipped through a lighthouse keeper to set the oven temperature.

'Do you mind?' she asked, as she sat down in the middle of a chambermaid.

Once the dough had risen, Jake popped it into the oven. It wasn't long before the lovely smell of baking bread filled the room. The ghosts were now drooling with anticipation. They closed in around the oven in a hotchpotch huddle of overlapping bodies.

'Is it ready yet?' they kept howling.

'Not yet,' said Granny firmly.

By the time the bread *was* ready, the ghosts were making such a din that no one heard the timer go off. But it didn't matter. The oven door was pushed open from inside and a little man sprang out.

Bread and Breakfast

The ghosts stopped howling and drew back as the little man, who was made from bread, advanced towards them.

'Come on then,' he said, 'who wants breakfast?'

There was an awkward silence. No one had expected the bread to be alive, let alone able to speak.

'Erm, if you don't mind me asking, what are you?' asked Jake.

'Don't you know?' said the little man. 'I'm a golem.'

'Oh,' said Jake, feeling no wiser, 'well, we're very pleased to meet you.'

'Well *I'd* be very pleased if you would *eat* me,' said the golem, 'before I get cold.'

'You actually want to be eaten?' asked Granny.

'Of course!' said the golem. 'Isn't that why you made me?'

'Well, yes,' said Jake, 'only we were expecting something a little more loaf-like.'

'Does it matter?' shrugged the golem. 'I want to be eaten anyway.'

'Are you sure?' asked Jake.

'Quite sure,' said the golem. 'Now is someone going to try me, or do I have to go outside and feed myself to the birds?'

Jake and Granny looked at the ghosts. They didn't seem so hungry all of a sudden. But Alexis cleared his throat and stepped forward.

'A good chef is always willing to experiment,' he said.

He picked up the golem and took a bite from one of its feet. Jake was relieved to see the mouthful vanish instead of falling to the floor.

'Hmm, very good!' said Alexis, chewing slowly. 'Very good indeed!'

'Thank you,' said the golem smiling.

'In fact –' said Alexis, grinning and patting his stomach. But before he could finish, he let out a big burp and vanished.

'It's done the trick,' said Granny.

As soon as the other ghosts saw this, they all began clamouring for a piece.

'One at a time,' said the golem. 'There's plenty of me to go round.'

Jake tried to form the ghosts into a queue, but they were so desperate, they kept jumping through each other until they all ended up in one squabbling blob at the front.

'This won't do,' said Granny. 'You can't all eat him at once. We'll start with whoever was born first.'

'That's me,' said Samuel eagerly, breaking off a piece of the golem and popping it into his mouth.

'Exquisite!' he pronounced, before vanishing with a burp.

One by one, each of the ghosts ate a piece of the golem, burped and then vanished. The bread seemed to work its magic quickest on the smaller ghosts, who disappeared instantly. The larger ghosts tended to sit around, smiling and rubbing their tummies for a while.

Trixibelle was the last to be fed, although she was by far the biggest ghost. By this time, only the golem's head was left.

'Cheerio!' said the little head, as Trixibelle stuffed it into her mouth.

'Yum-yum!' said Trixibelle, as she chewed contentedly.

'She's the only one left,' said Granny, looking around her. 'Let's just hope she vanishes before the police get here.'

But Trixibelle didn't vanish. She fell asleep on top of the kitchen table and was still lying there, snoring happily, when the doorbell rang.

'That's the police,' gasped Granny. 'What are we going to do?'

'You stall them,' said Jake, 'while I wake her up and hide her.'

Granny opened the front door a crack. Snatchett was standing outside with a police inspector and a policewoman.

'Hello,' said Granny politely. 'Can I help you?'

'Yes, you can let us in,' said Snatchett rudely, trying to push past her.

'Why?' asked Granny innocently.

'You know why, you old witch,' said Snatchett. 'You've been raising the dead and these officers are here to arrest you.'

'Now hold on a minute, sir,' said the police inspector. 'I'm afraid we'll need some evidence first.'

'You'll find plenty inside,' snapped Snatchett. 'Now, tell her to let us in.'

'If you *would* be so kind, madam,' said the policewoman.

Granny stood aside reluctantly and Snatchett scuttled past her into the cottage.

The police officers shuffled in after him. They felt a bit silly. Neither of them believed in ghosts. They were only there because Snatchett was so rich and important, they had to pretend to take him seriously.

Granny crossed her fingers and hoped that Trixibelle had found somewhere to hide.

Goodbye Mr Snatchett

Trixibelle wasn't hiding. She was still fast asleep.

Jake couldn't prod or shake her awake because his hands went right through her. And when he tried shouting in her ear she just sighed and rolled over.

There was no time left so he decided to try and hide her where she lay. He threw one of Granny's tablecloths over her, but it dropped straight through her onto the table.

So she was still lying there, in full view, when Snatchett shot into the kitchen a moment later.

'In here,' Snatchett shouted, 'on the table.

A ghost! I told you. Come and see.'

The police officers, who were still standing in the hall, shrugged at each other and followed Snatchett into the kitchen.

The instant before they entered the room, Trixibelle rolled over, let out an enormous belch and vanished.

'Pardon me,' said Jake, slapping his chest as the officers looked in his direction.

'Did you see it! Did you see it!' shouted Snatchett.

'It's a small boy,' said the inspector.

'He doesn't look much like a ghost,' remarked the policewoman. Neither of them had seen Trixibelle.

'Not him,' snapped Snatchett. 'The big fat one! The ballet-dancer! You must have seen her, she was enormous.'

'A big fat ballet-dancing ghost?' said the inspector.

'Yes!' said Snatchett, nodding furiously.

'I see,' said the inspector, giving the policewoman a wink.

'Go on then,' said Snatchett pointing at Granny. 'Arrest her.'

'Has this gentleman been bothering you for long, madam?' asked the policewoman, taking out her notebook.

'Yes,' said Granny, 'he and his friend have been hanging around here for weeks.'

'Well, I dare say he won't be bothering you any longer,' said the inspector, pulling a pair of handcuffs out of his pocket.

'Not once you're in prison!' sneered Snatchett.

'No, not once *you're* in prison, sir,' corrected the inspector, fastening the handcuffs around Snatchett's wrists.

'What are you doing?' demanded Snatchett. 'She's the one that's breaking the law!'

'I hardly think so, sir,' said the policewoman, pulling him towards the door. 'You ought to be ashamed of yourself, harassing this harmless old lady.'

'Wait a minute,' pleaded Snatchett. 'I

haven't told you about the flying saucepan or the soup flood.'

'Yes, yes,' said the policewoman, rolling her eyes. 'You can tell us all about them on the way to the station.'

'Sorry about this,' said the inspector, on his way out. 'We thought his story sounded a bit funny, but if we'd known that he was this potty we wouldn't have bothered you. As it is, I can assure you he won't be troubling you again.'

'That's marvellous,' said Granny. 'I'd be so grateful.'

'Think nothing of it,' said the inspector. 'It's the least we can do.'

'Good riddance to bad rubbish!' said Jake as he watched Snatchett being driven off in the police car.

'You don't think anyone will believe him, do you?' asked Granny as she cleaned up the kitchen.

'Not for a minute,' said Jake. 'Not even if they knew the *whole* story.'

'I suppose you're right,' said Granny, grinning as she put The Conjuror's Cookbook back on its shelf. 'Talking bread, shrieking sauce, ghosts that swim out of your mouth . . .

. . . A story like that would have to have been *cooked up*!'

Golem Bread

As The Conjuror's Cookbook says, *proper*
Golem Bread is 'too insubstantial for the human
stomach'. Its texture is so light and its flavour so
delicate that you wouldn't notice that you were
eating it.

This recipe is for bread that you'll enjoy eating
– although it won't be able to talk to you! **But
make sure you get a grown-up to help you bake
it!**

INGREDIENTS
350 g (12 oz) **Plain Flour**
1 Teaspoon of **Salt**
1 Teaspoon (*½ a sachet*) **Easy-Blend Yeast**
225 ml (8 fl oz) **Warm Water**
A little **Butter, Margarine** <u>OR</u> **Oil** for
greasing.

Mix the flour, salt and yeast together
thoroughly in a large bowl. Then add the water
gradually while mixing with a wooden spoon.
Finish off the mixing with your hands, squeezing

the dough together until it is soft but not sticky.

Sprinkle some extra flour onto a work surface and place the dough onto it. Now it needs *kneading*! Flatten the dough under the heel of your hand, then fold it in half, give it a quarter turn (clockwise or anticlockwise) and then flatten it again. Keep flattening, folding and turning for about 10 minutes until the dough is smooth and springy. Kneading is quite hard work, but it's important to do it thoroughly, so if you get tired, get your grown-up to finish it or take a rest before carrying on.

Put the dough into a greased bowl and cover with a clean tea towel. Then leave it in a warm place (such as an airing cupboard or a troll's armpit) for an hour until it has doubled in size, or *risen*. If you don't have a warm place, then leave it for 2 hours at room temperature.

Meanwhile, preheat the oven to gas mark 8, 230° C (450°F).

When the dough has risen you can shape it into a golem. Flatten the dough into a circle about 18cm wide and then push five deep dents into the edge to make a flower shape as shown. Pull out and shape four of the flower's petals to make the golem's arm and legs and pinch a neck in the fifth petal to make his head. Use your fingers to poke deep holes for the eyes and mouth.

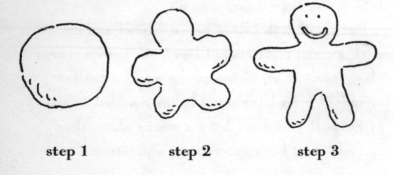

step 1   step 2   step 3

Place the golem on a well-greased baking sheet and bake at the top of the oven for 30 minutes until brown. Remove with oven gloves and leave to cool on a wire rack. But don't leave it for too long before eating it, you don't want to hurt its feelings!